HALLOWEEN BOOK FESTIVAL 2013

* * *

TERROR AT THE TAILOR'S...

The front door swung open; out of the storm and into the shop rushed Gretl, blonde braids awhirl. "Oopsy, forgot my umbrel—" Then she froze.

All eyes—her father's, Ygor's, and the Monster's—shot over to her.

"Daughter!" Klaus commanded. "Get out!"

But the girl, gaze locked on the looming Monster, rushed bravely forward, stopping where her father knelt. "Are—are you all right? Papa, what *is* that?"

A crackle of lightning outside as, fingers groping the air, the creature advanced on her.

A great *BOOM* of thunder as Ygor nodded and cackled.

Klaus jumped to his feet and pushed his daughter behind him. For lack of a weapon, he whisked his sewing mannequin off the counter, hoisting the wire torso like a bludgeon.

The Monster yanked the false figure away from the tailor—and tore it in two.

Klaus watched the dummy halves clatter to the floor.

"Ye-e-e-es!" Ygor hissed, his face lightning-lit. "See what my friend can do? Now, he do same to tailor-man." Ygor pointed at Klaus. "You no make 'major alterations' on suit, *Herr* Hauptschmidt; my friend here make zem—on *you!*"

Also by Paul McComas:

Unforgettable:
Harrowing Futures, Horrors, & (Dark) Humor

Planet of the Dates

Unplugged

Twenty Questions

First Person Imperfect (editor)

Further Persons Imperfect (editor)

FIT FOR A FRANKENSTEIN

A novella by

It's an honor to meet your Honor!

Paul McComas

&

Greg Starrett

TO THE MAYOR
"FRIEND GOOOOOOD"

Walkabout Publishing • 2013

Walkabout Publishing
S.D. Studios
P.O. Box 151
Kansasville, WI 53139
www.walkaboutpublishing.com

© 2013 by Paul McComas and Greg Starrett.
Cover by Nick Endres.
Authors' photo by Laurie Starrett; makeup by Greg Starrett.

All rights reserved, including the right of reproduction in whole or in part in any form. No part of this publication may be reproduced or transmitted in any form or by any means, electronic or mechanical, including photocopying, recording, scanning, or any information storage and retrieval system, without written permission of the authors.

First Edition, February 2013
Second Edition, January 2014

Printed in the U.S.A.

ISBN: 978-1-4826-2233-1

ACKNOWLEDGMENTS

FROM PAUL:

Thanks to my wife, Heather, for L & P (love and proofreading); to my mom and, in memoriam, dad for their indulgence throughout my childhood-long Monster Phase; to my website maven, Neal Katz; to my publicist, Liz Ridley; and to John Scott, who was and is—along with Greg—the best "monster buddy" a guy could hope to have.

FROM GREG:

I wish to thank my wife Laurie, our daughter Stacy, and my parents, all of whom have given me love and support for so many years. A special thanks to my other "monster friend," Scott Merkel; friend and monster fan Casey Sullivan; and childhood "monster pals" Roy Augun, the late Paul Augun, Chris and Bryan Nagle, and Rob and Kim Wagner.

FROM BOTH:

Deep thanks to our publisher, Steve Sullivan, for his alert editorial eye—and for making our crazy dream come true; to illustrator Nick Endres for cover art worth far more than the meager sum proffered; and to 1930s and '40s Universal Pictures for the inspiration!

For Bela,

Lon Jr.,

Boris...

and Forry

CONTENTS

1. Ill Suited for Travel 13

2. What's Bad for the Goose Is Good for the Monster 17

3. All Those Years Ago 23

4. Kotstadt or Büst 29

5. Enter: The Tailor 31

6. Away in a Manger 40

7. Meanwhile, Back at Hauptschmidt Tailors.....................43

8. Das Heist 46

9. All-Nighter 49

10. Vhat Dreams May Come 51

11. Asleep at the Wheel 58

12. Major Alter(c)ations..61

13. On Ze Road Again 70

Authors' Note 73

Bonus story: "After the Fall" (a.k.a. "Living Ghost")..........81

About the Authors..85

"When Ygor and the Monster leave the village of Frankenstein, Ygor tells the Monster that they will go to see [Dr.] Ludwig [Frankenstein, in the town of Vasaria], who will give the Monster back his strength ... We are not shown how they get to Vasaria, [but] Ygor looks pretty disheveled—who wouldn't be, with a few bullet holes in him?—and the Monster, caked in dried sulfur, looks like the stuff from which nightmares are made. (**Ygor, however, has managed to get the Monster cleaned up and gotten him a new suit by the time the weird-looking pair enters Vasaria.**)"

(Emphasis added)
From Leonard J. Kohl's essay on the film
The Ghost of Frankenstein in the
Midnight Marquee Actors Series book
Lon Chaney, Jr. (1997, Luminary Press)

VUN
ILL SUITED FOR TRAVEL

At long last, the wicked November storm was subsiding; the rain and lightning had ceased, but the night wind remained, whistling in Ygor's ears as he staggered out of the brush into the vacant, muddy road. There in front of him, on the other side, stood what appeared to be a wooden sign.

He stepped closer, chin raised, eyes squinting to make out the shape:

Not a single sign, but *two*: arrow-shaped, one above the other, nailed to a post—and pointing in two different directions.

Ygor turned back toward the brush—no small feat: his broken neck made over-the-shoulder glances impossible. Yes, he had somehow managed to walk away, years ago, from his rendezvous with the gallows, but the botched execution had rendered him incapable of rotating his head. So instead, he had to pivot from the waist, the entire upper half of his body swiveling grotesquely to one side.

"Is fork in ze road!" he rasped at the bushes from which he'd emerged. "Ygor vill see vhich vay ve go."

No reply from the shadowy figure hulking in the brush.

Ygor turned back to the signage and took a few steps toward it. He read aloud the words carved into both directional arrows: first, the top one, which was pointing to the northwest...

Harnstadt, 4 Km

...then the bottom one, pointing to the northeast:

Kotstadt, 11 Km
Vasaria, 48 Km

Ygor grimaced. "Is no good," he mumbled to himself. "Ve need food, shelter, place to rest. Harnstadt closer ... but is wrong direction." He sighed mightily, then turned, again, back to the bushes. "Ve go to Kotstadt!" he barked. "Zen, to Vasaria. But ve use road, like men—not crash through voods like animals. Come!" And he motioned with two jerks of his arm.

The shadow in the brush shifted but did not emerge.

Ygor shuffled halfway back to the foliage. "Ygor know," he croaked, nodding. "You afraid—not vant to be seen. But, is dark and stormy night; road is empty. No vun vill see us now." He gestured again. "Come!"

A moment later, the bushes split open with a sharp *CRACK*, and out into a shaft of moonlight stepped ... a nightmare. It loomed high and wide, swaying a bit, massive arms held out to its sides, vacant eyes staring, and the whole of it nearly glowing like a ghastly moon against the black sky: a sickly-white, sulfur-caked abomination.

The Monster.

Ygor scowled; he scratched idly at his scruffy beard. "Maybe ... maybe zis not such a good idea. You still coated vhite, from ze pit; you stick out like sore thumb!"

The Monster, confused but eager to oblige, raised its right hand, opposable digit pointing up.

"No, no; is just expression." Ygor stepped up to the creature and pushed its arm back down—then raised his own palm, eyeing the chalky residue. He brought his hand to his nose, sniffed it—"Is like ze rotten eggs"—then sniffed again ... and grimaced. "No: is more like ze gruel they serve at

Fit for a Frankenstein

Frankenshtein Prison, on ze death row!" Savagely, Ygor wiped his palm against his trouser leg, then peered up at the Monster: "I vish you still vearing your old black suit, *vithout* ze sulfur; zen, ve could travel by night and stay hidden. No vun see you, no vun smell you, and no vun ze viser. But, like *zis...*"

The Monster dipped its chin, staring mutely down at itself.

Ygor's tone softened: "No ... no. Is not your fault, my friend." He patted his companion once, twice on the back. "Ygor make better for you. Ve go through ze voods, to Kotstadt. Ve find place zhere to vash your clothes, maybe use ze dry-cleaning to get ze sulfur out, and—" His eyes widened, and he smiled. "No! No: ve find tailor-man, make *new* suit for you, heh-heh! You like zat, eh?"

The Monster said nothing.

"Yeeesss, new suit, *brand* new; Ygor see to it. Ygor dress you good as new, so vhen ve get to Vasaria and find Ludvig, ze second son of Frankenshtein, he take vun look at you, and he velcome you vith open arms, like ... like long-lost baby brother!"

The Monster blinked.

Ygor chuckled. "You know vhat zey say? 'Clothes make ze man.' So? Clothes just like Frankenshtein, eh? *He* make ze man, too: *you!* Heh-heh-heh."

The Monster didn't get it.

Ygor took hold of its massive arm. "You come," he instructed, and pulled the creature back into the brush. "Is not so far, my friend; Ygor lead ze vay." Heading northeast, he slipped between night-black trees that groaned and creaked in the howling wind, the Monster two paces behind him. "Ve go through voods. Ve go to Kotstadt. And zhere, Ygor get you fine, new suit—"

Paul McComas & Greg Starrett

In the distance: a rumble of thunder.

"—suit vorthy to be vorn by ... a Frankenshtein!"

TWO
WHAT'S BAD FOR THE GOOSE IS GOOD FOR THE MONSTER

After hours of walking through the dark forest, stumbling over rocks and fallen logs that they could not see in the blackness, the faint light of dawn was a welcome sight. Now able to step more safely, Ygor and the Monster found themselves traveling at a quicker pace. "Is better now, eh?" said Ygor, ducking around a dead tree trunk. "Ze light, it help Ygor keep going, even zhough he is tired. And *you*—" He jabbed a thumb back toward his towering familiar. "You no get tired, *ever!*"

The Monster, reaching the same dead tree trunk, swept it aside; with a crackling *thud*, it crashed to the ground.

"No, you no get tired. Ygor only hope you never get tired of *him!* Heh-heh-heh."

The Monster gave him a blank look.

After an hour, the sun was much higher in the sky. Ygor gestured toward a small clearing off to the right: "Ve stop here to rest, catch breath."

They sat down on a pair of moss-covered stumps, and it was then, in the resulting silence, that Ygor heard something off in the distance. He cupped his hand to his ear, and his eyes widened; his voice was a harsh whisper: "Listen, my friend. Listen."

The Monster imitated Ygor, placing a hand beside its own ear; its massive head pivoted one way and then the other, straining toward the sound.

"You hear zat? Hear ze honking? It is ze vild geeses."

The Monster looked confused.

17

Paul McComas & Greg Starrett

Ygor reached over and grabbed the Monster by one sulfurous sleeve. "Don't you see? Ve eat zem, my friend. Ze geeses—zey are food!"

The Monster turned toward the sound, his lips curling into a twisted grin. Delivered mere hours ago from his encasement in the sulfur pit, he hadn't eaten in years—literally.

"Come," said Ygor, clambering back to his feet. "Ve go to ze geeses."

They left the clearing and followed the sound down a steep hill. Near the bottom, Ygor could see the bright reflection of sunlight on the surface of a pond. A few steps later, he was able to make out a small flock of geese swimming in placid, lazy circles. He hurried down to the shore and made a clumsy attempt to grab the nearest bird by its long neck—almost falling into the pond in the process. "Ze goose," he lamented, righting himself, "it is too fast for old Ygor. Come, my friend: *you* try."

The Monster wasted no time doing what his friend had asked: he lumbered into the water, right into the middle of the loudly protesting flock, grabbed a goose by the neck, and gave it one quick shake.

That was all it took.

Ygor laughed and clapped his hands. "Yes, yes!"

The Monster threw the goose onto the shore, right by Ygor's feet.

"You are fine hunter, my friend!" Ygor bent down and scooped up the dead bird; he squeezed it, admiring its plumpness. "Is good. You go, get us anozher. Meanvhile, Ygor make fire and cook your goose."

As the Monster turned back toward the pond, Ygor began gathering up some sticks and dry leaves, plus a good-sized rock. Then he arranged what he'd retrieved into a small

Fit for a Frankenstein

heap, removed the flint from his deerskin shoulder-pouch, and soon had a cooking-fire started.

Warming his hands before the crackling flames, he heard the Monster coming toward him through the brush. Ygor looked up to see that his friend—a second, even plumper goose clutched in his right hand—was now clean from the waist down. "Ze water, it took ze sulfur off you, didn't it?"

The Monster looked confused.

Ygor pointed at its legs—"Half black"—then raised his finger. "And half vhite. You look like vun of ze two-tone cookies Ygor used to steal—er, zey *said*—from behind ze counter of ze Frankenshtein Bakery!" And he began to laugh his raspy, bone-in-the-throat laugh.

His companion dropped the goose. Hands raised, staring down at itself, the Monster looked vaguely hurt.

Ygor stood, shaking his head—but still grinning wide. "Ha! Is all right; Ygor just play vith you, just ... just tease. Come; come. Ve go back to ze vater and finish ze job." And he led the Monster out of the clearing.

At the shore of the pond, Ygor folded his arms, then wrinkled his nose. "Ygor hate to say zis, my friend, but vith ze sulfur and ze sweat, right now you have stench"—he waved a hand in front of his own face—"stench of a hundred men! Go," he said, shooing the Monster off. "You valk into ze vater. It vill vash you clean."

The Monster looked at Ygor, and then at the water: there were no geese left, for the rest of the flock had fled. The Monster stood immobile, staring at the pond's surface.

"Go, my friend, into ze vater—and zen, ve vill eat."

The thought of eating made the Monster more cooperative, and it began wading in.

"Keep going," said Ygor with a crooked nod. "Deeper ... deeper into ze pond."

19

Paul McComas & Greg Starrett

The Monster kept walking and was soon in up to its neck; Ygor watched the nearer of its two electrodes catch a ray of sunlight and then dip under the surface. An ever-growing cloud of sulfur stained the water all around the Monster. "Is far enough," croaked Ygor with a smile—but then his expression turned to one of horror as the Monster's head disappeared beneath the surface.

He bolted forward, standing ankle-deep in the pond. "No, *no*, my friend—come back!" Ygor's eyes scanned the pond, looking for a trace of movement ... but there was nothing.

His withered old heart pounded in his chest. A frog croaked; songbirds chirped; but the water remained deathly still.

A full minute passed. Still nothing.

Finally, a few faint ripples appeared, more than halfway across the pond. The flat top of the Monster's great head broke through the surface, moving into shallower water as the creature strode slowly, steadily toward the opposite shore.

Ygor sighed in relief, then raised his voice: "You valk all ze vay, straight across ze bottom of ze pond! Didn't you?"

The Monster reached the shore and turned around—his ragged clothes now shiny-black and sulfur-free.

"You no two-tone cookie *now*, are you? Heh-heh-heh. And, look!" Ygor pointed to the center of the pond, where three trout bobbed, belly-up, near the surface. "Ze sulfur, it kill ze fishes—bring us some 'surf' to go vith our 'turf.' My friend," he laughed, "you not only good hunter; you also fine fisherman!"

The Monster stared at the floating corpses.

"You come back here now, and"—Ygor pointed—"you pick up ze fishes along ze vay."

The Monster complied.

20

Fit for a Frankenstein

When at last it strode back onto the shore from whence it had departed, the Monster grabbed Ygor by the arm—then tapped its own stomach with a fistful of fish.

"Yes, my friend," Ygor said with a nod. "Now, ve eat."

They returned to the cooking-fire, now blazing away. Ygor demonstrated how to pluck the feathers from the geese—at this, the Monster proved to be a natural—then pulled the hunting knife from his pouch and deftly cleaned the trio of trout. In no time at all, fish and fowl alike were impaled on small branches and crackling away. The Monster drew a deep breath into its nostrils, savoring the aroma ... but eyed the flames warily, no doubt because *"Fire baaad."*

"How you like it, eh?" Ygor asked. "How you like meat?"

The Monster appeared confused.

"Medium-rare"—he gestured toward their meal-in-process—"like now? Or medium? Vell done?"

In answer, the Monster grabbed a great, bulbous drumstick, tore it out of the bird's hip joint, drew the leg quickly to its mouth and sank its teeth in deep, grinding and devouring meat and bone alike.

His companion nodded—"Ygor like medium-rare, too"—and helped himself to the other drumstick.

They both ate with abandon. But partway into their feast, the Monster stopped.

Ygor, tossing aside a fish head, peered up. "You full?"

Slowly, the Monster shook its head.

"Vhat, zen? Ze geeses and ze trout-fish, zey not enough?"

The Monster looked off into the woods.

"You vish to eat something else—something in zhere?" Ygor was growing annoyed. "You vant maybe venison, or ze morel mushrooms? Ze vild honey? Here..." He grabbed a scrap of bloody goose-down and shoved it at the Monster; Ygor's voice was loud now, his tone sarcastic: "Here is menu!

21

Paul McComas & Greg Starrett

Let Ygor describe Daily Specials. You vant he should tell you about ze *rabbits?* Gorge!"—he tossed the Monster a trout— "Gorge yourself on ze fish and ze goose; is all ve have today! How much you *pay* for zis meal anyvay, eh?"

The Monster looked down at the ground, its immense shoulders drooping in shame.

Ygor instantly regretted his words. "No ... no; Ygor not mean it. You good fellow, good friend—Ygor's *only* friend. Ygor sorry." And he reached out his hand in consolation.

The Monster pushed it away.

"No ... please. Ygor forget zat you no can talk, no can tell him vhat you vant. Is hard for Ygor—but is harder for you." He tried again, clamping his palm around the Monster's arm.

This time, the Monster let it stay.

"Good, is good!" Ygor nearly sang, nodding. "Ve friends again!" Then, with his free hand, he reached toward the fire for a thick, wide, succulent slab of breast meat—the prime cut—and made of it a peace offering.

The Monster downed it in a single bite.

A short while later, Ygor lay back in the soft marsh grass, hands folded atop his full stomach, and let out a yawn.

Beside him sat the Monster—and a sizable pile of bones.

"Zat vas good feast, eh, my friend?"

The Monster grunted in agreement.

"Let us rest a vhile, before ve set off for Kotstadt."

The Monster lay back, too. Its clothes were finally beginning to dry out from its stroll along the bottom of the pond.

The duo soon fell fast asleep in the warm midday sun.

THREE
ALL THOSE YEARS AGO

Ygor glanced around, unsure of where he was. He saw a splintery wooden bench standing on an uneven, cracked stone floor. His head tilted up: set at face height into the grey brick wall was a small window with rusty iron bars. It all *looked* familiar enough—yet it was the odor of fetid water and human waste that jarred his memory ... then knotted his stomach.

The cell.

He knew this place well. *Too* well. For it was not just any cell, but the death-row cell where the Chief Magistrate and his henchmen had held Ygor after his trial and conviction for the crime of grave robbing, back in the village of Frankenstein. After his trial, and before his—

Bang ... bang ... bang...

"A hammer?" he muttered to himself, and stood on tiptoes to look out the window:

Ygor's eyes went wide. For there, in the middle of the village square, three workmen were constructing a gallows.

His voice sank to a whimper: "Zey vill hang Ygor in ze morning."

In self-defense, his mind raced back, back, to an earlier, safer time and place:

...Here, again, was the illustrious Dr. Heinrich Frankenstein, hands clasped behind him, ambling into Ygor's run-down blacksmith shop. "I see," Frankenstein casually began, "that your business has fallen off since that *new* smith opened, down the street."

23

Paul McComas & Greg Starrett

"Yes, *Herr Doktor*. It has hurt Ygor, right vhere it counts"—he patted the leather pouch hanging from his hip—"in ze pocketbook."

The doctor unclasped his hands and folded his arms. "What if I could offer you twice what you earn here in a whole month, just to do a little work for me?"

"And vhat kind of work vould cause a rich man like Frankenshtein"—here, Ygor reached out and stroked the fine fabric of the doctor's expensive navy-blue suit—"to offer so many of his precious *marks t*o Ygor?"

"Nothing much, really—just a quiet visit to the graveyard at night, to obtain a few ... specimens."

"You mean *bodies*, don't you, Frankenshtein? You vant Ygor to steal bodies. Vhat makes you think Ygor vould do something like zat?"

"Let's just say you have the reputation of being a man who's willing to do *anything*—as long as it pays."

Ygor gave his visitor a sly smile, then nodded. "Yes, *Herr Doktor*; Ygor vill do it. But you vill pay him *four* times vhat he earns in a month."

Frankenstein nodded in agreement, and the deal was made ... a deal that would land Ygor—

"Here, in ze cell—I'm back in ze cell. It's all happening again!" Ygor shook his shaggy head. "But *how?*"

The long, lonely night offered no answers...

Dawn. The condemned man gazed out through bars into the breaking light of a new day.

His last day.

Ygor heard the echo of heavy footsteps in the corridor. *Approaching* footsteps. "Z-zey are coming for Ygor," he stammered, "t-to hang him!" The cell door creaked open; two guards burst in and grabbed him firmly by the arms—yet the younger of the two, Ygor noticed, himself appeared to have

24

Fit for a Frankenstein

but *one* arm. "Vhat?" the prisoner blustered. "A vun-armed guard is vhat Ygor get?"

"You try and escape," the youthful *gendarme* retorted, "and you'll see how quickly my one arm strikes you down!"

"Come on, Krogh," muttered his partner. "Don't let this ghoul get your goat. He'll be dead in a few minutes anyway."

Together, they dragged Ygor out of his cell, through the prison yard and, under a corpse-grey sky, into the village square. His heart pounded in his chest as he peered up and saw, atop the gallows, the black-hooded hangman reaching to adjust the noose that soon would embrace Ygor's neck.

Hustled through the crowd, the prisoner gazed around in desperation at the gathered villagers and saw among them many familiar faces: Lang ... Neumuller ... Lieber ... Reifsteck ... Fidorf ... Krauthammer ... Reinhardt ... and Merkel: all eight of the esteemed town *Burghers* who had judged him guilty. Looking away from their burning eyes, he heard the hateful cries of the crowd:

"Accursed fiend!"

"Body snatcher!"

"Grave robber!"

"*Devil!*"

Ygor peered down at his own feet and watched them ascend the rickety steps: right, left, right, left. The instant he reached the top, the noose was slipped over his head, quickly followed by a black hood. Unlike the hangman's, this one had no eye holes; Ygor saw nothing now, but he heard the *Burghermeister* reading the guilty verdict and the pronounced sentence. Then he heard a loud *WHAM* as the trapdoor beneath his feet swung open and he plunged down and a jolt of pain *tore* through his neck and then—

Nothing.

"Cut the body down," the *Burghermeister* directed.

Paul McComas & Greg Starrett

The hangman deployed his skinning knife and, with three deft strokes, severed the rope:

Ygor's corpse hit the ground with a *thud*.

The town coroner approached it, knelt, and removed the hood, revealing to one and all the grisly evidence of a snapped neck. The portly physician checked for a pulse—but only briefly; after all, the results were self-evident:

"I pronounce this man dead."

As the doctor turned away and the crowd dispersed, a cold rain began to fall.

The two remaining villagers pulled a small wagon up to where the body lay. They removed the noose; then, taking hold of wrists and ankles, they hoisted the corpse off the ground.

It had been decided at his trial that Ygor's crime of body snatching made burial in a church yard or cemetery impossible; no holy place could receive the corpse of so despicable a sinner. Rather, the *Burghers* had decided, the deceased belonged in an *un*holy place, and the most unholy place in the village was where all the evil had started: the Frankenstein estate. Ygor's corpse was to be unceremoniously dumped into the ruins of the Doctor's laboratory, where the fiendish Monster had been assembled and then given life.

The two unlucky villagers who had been stuck with the task—the ones manning the wagon—trembled with fear as they transported Ygor's body to its final resting place. Even though the Monster was said to have been destroyed when it blew up the laboratory via a conveniently placed lever, no one was certain that the threat had passed. After all, the creature had survived being trapped in a burning windmill; perhaps it could just as easily walk out of an explosion? The trembling

Fit for a Frankenstein

twosome therefore took no chances, quickly throwing Ygor's corpse off the cart.

As his body hit the ground ... Ygor *felt* it! The impact woke him, perhaps not from death but from something close to it, and caused the former smith to resume breathing—albeit with difficulty: the effort made him cough.

The men with the cart both thought they'd heard something. Too afraid to look behind them, they glanced briefly at one another—then hurried back to the safety of their homes in the village.

Slowly, painfully, Ygor gathered himself up. Crooked, misshapen, and trembling spasmodically, he somehow stood. He looked around the ruins of the laboratory and saw a trickle of water falling through one of the many gaping holes in the structure's roof. He was terribly thirsty, so he turned and stumbled toward the thin stream; he had only made it a few steps, though, before he collapsed to the ground. Weakened by his ordeal, and unable to breathe freely, he now found that, try as he might, he was no longer able to stand. He extended his hand toward the trickle, but it was just out of reach. "Vater," he gasped. "Vater!"

Then he heard a sound. *Is ... rat?* Or was someone else here, moving around in the ruins? A massive shadow passed over Ygor's face; "Zat," he muttered, "is no rat!" Ygor struggled to roll onto his back, whereupon he found himself looking up at...

Ze Monster?

Yes; it had to be! Although Ygor had helped procure parts for its creation, he had never actually seen the fearsome, flat-headed giant before. Ygor lay helpless as a huge hand grabbed him by the shoulder and lifted him off the ground. "No, no!" he yelled. "Leave me alone!"

27

Paul McComas & Greg Starrett

The Monster gently set him down against a rock—right under the trickle of water.

Ygor drank greedily, water splashing in his face, as the Monster watched. After he'd had his fill, he turned to face his benefactor. "Thank you ... my friend." Ygor struggled upward, stood—but his legs gave way and he began to fall. At the edge of consciousness, he felt himself being caught by two enormous arms, and he heard the creature croak out two words:

"Friend ... goooood."

FOUR
KOTSTADT OR BÜST

Ygor awoke from the dream with a smile on his face, for what had started out as the recurring nightmare of his execution had gone further than usual, taking a turn for the better.

Rubbing the sleep from his eyes, he became aware of a sound: something big, splashing around in the nearby water. "Is probably vhat voke me up," he muttered to himself, then looked over to see if his companion had heard it too, but the Monster was—*gone?* Ygor jumped to his feet and looked in alarm toward the pond, only to see:

The Monster, waist-deep, breaking the neck of yet another goose.

Ygor sighed in exasperated relief, then shook his head. "You doing zat for fun, my friend? Or you still hungry, after such a meal as ve had?"

The Monster placed his free hand to his belly.

"Come vith Ygor; ve vill find *many* good things to eat in town. Maybe even ze thing you vanted before." Then, under his breath: "Vhatever ze hell *zat* vas!"

The Monster started toward Ygor, still clutching the goose.

"Come, my friend; come vith me. Is not far now..."

Ygor was right, for within the hour they stood on a rolling hillside, gazing down into the valley below. There, amidst vivid-hued fall foliage, a two-steepled church was surrounded by a smattering of one- and two-story buildings, comprising a tiny alpine village—the town of Kotstadt.

29

Paul McComas & Greg Starrett

"Zat's it. Zat's *it!*" Again, Ygor reached up and clamped his hand around the Monster's arm—but this time, the threadbare black fabric tore clean off the creature's bicep.

The Monster stared down at its own freshly exposed green-grey skin.

Ygor's mouth and eyes went wide. "Oh, no! Vhat I do?" He struggled in vain to wrap the scrap back around the Monster's bare arm, but only succeeded in tearing his friend's jacket in front—revealing one flat grey nipple.

The Monster unleashed a low, wordless snarl.

Ygor, hands raised, took a step back. "All right; Ygor no touch." He dropped the scrap, then folded his arms and peered at the Monster's apparel, taking stock. "Ze pants—zey just as bad: about to come apart in two, three places." He nodded. "Is all ze vear-and-tear. Ze sulfur pit, ze light-en-ing hitting you, ze long valk through ze voods, ze in-and-out-of-ze-pond..." Ygor shook his head in disgust. "Is all too much for ze cut-rate clothes Frankenshtein shtick you in!" Then his tone turned sympathetic: "Just because you made from bodies dug out of ze dirt, zat no reason to dress you dirt cheap."

The Monster was poking at its own bare arm with the fingertips of its other hand, its expression one of confused fascination.

Ygor stepped forward. "You ... you never see your own flesh before. Do you?"

The Monster shook its head.

"Vell, ve get you into Kotstadt, and ve find you tailor, right away." Ygor began heading down the hillside, beckoning his companion to follow. "Otvervise, ve both going to be seeing a lot *more* of your flesh very soon—more, my friend, zan Ygor vish to see!"

30

FIVE
ENTER: THE TAILOR

Klaus Hauptschmidt, one month shy of forty and feeling far older, straightened the knot of his silk necktie, then reached past his well-worn volume of Sigmund Freud's *Civilization and Its Discontents* to pluck from atop his bureau the handkerchief that matched his cravat. After folding the glossy cloth into a triangle and slipping it curtly into his tweed jacket's breast pocket, he paused; standing there in front of what once had been his great-grandparents' oaken wall mirror, he regarded his reflection:

The high forehead, he'd been told, denoted intellect and taste—two qualities on which this rural-born aesthete and self-driven scholar prided himself, perhaps above all others ... but the receding hairline indicated stress. *Yes,* thought Klaus, *and discontent with what passes, here, for "civilization."* The square chin meant strength ... but the nervous, darting blue eyes spoke of uncertainty. "Quite the mixed bag," he muttered. "Little wonder so many have doubted me!" His gaze rose to the sepia-tone photographic portrait that stood, in gilded frame, behind the Freud book. "Not my dear Seidel, though," Klaus reminded himself. "She always believed." Then his eyes shifted higher still, toward the heavens: "God keep you, *Liebchen.*"

But the shouted answer came from *below*: "Are you there?"

Her voice! Klaus, shaken, placed a hand to the wall. "S-Seidelbast?" he stammered.

"No, *Vater.* It's me."

Paul McComas & Greg Starrett

Klaus sighed. Of course: it was their treasured daughter, their only child, calling up the steps from the shop below. The girl's voice sounded just like that of her sainted mother—and Gretl *looked* so much like Seidel-at-17, too—that sometimes, Klaus found himself momentarily disoriented. The resemblance was both blessing and curse. He cleared his throat. "Yes, I'm up here, Gretl, dear. What do you need?"

"*Vater*, I think we have a customer."

A customer? Klaus saw himself smile, for this was welcome news indeed; to call business of late "slow" would have been generous. "Things are looking up!" he told his reflection, then gave it a wink and turned toward the stairs.

Gretl—appearing more woman than girl in her crisp, white, bunched-at-the-elbows blouse and knee-length blue dirndl skirt—met him halfway up the steps. One of her two long blonde braids had worked its way in front of her shoulder; she flipped it behind her and peered up at her papa with anxious eyes.

But why? She should be delighted, just as he was! "*Damen? Herren?*"

"It's ... a man."

Klaus shook his head. "What troubles you, *Tochter*?"

"It's ... the man."

"What of him?"

She pointed mutely down the stairs.

"Did you speak to him?"

She shook her head. "I was ... afraid to."

"Fine. Let us have a *look* at this man"—his voice had edged into impatience—"this man, Gretl, who comes, thanks be to *Gott*, to spend his *marks* at Hauptschmidt Tailors!" He placed a palm on her small shoulder, then moved briskly past her, down the rest of the steps, and through the back work

Fit for a Frankenstein

area of his shop, asking himself: *What* will *you find out there, tailor?*

The surprising answer that popped, unbidden, into Klaus' head: *Your destiny.*

He stepped out from behind the curtains and up to the front counter. "Sir, may I hel—?"

"Hel" was as far as he got. *Appropriate,* thought Klaus with a chill—for surely *Hölle* itself must have spawned the grinning creature now standing before him.

"You Hauptschmidt ze tailor?" The voice was like broken fingernails on sandpaper.

Klaus steadied himself and answered firmly: "I am."

"You ze best tailor in Kotstadt?"

He repeated: "I am." And thought: *Also the* only *tailor in Kotstadt.*

His unseemly visitor glanced around the sparse front room. "Ygor ... not see very many clothes. Vhy not more business?"

"Well..." Klaus hesitated.

The visitor continued: "Ygor vorked as blacksmith vunce, *Herr* Hauptschmidt. Shop *alvays* full of jobs needing to be done—horseshoes, gates, grilles, veapons..."

"Yes, well," Klaus replied, "how very lovely for you. Unfortunately, the people of this fair burg prefer to make, mend, and alter their *own* apparel." He glanced out the window to the street. "Even if it does leave them looking, more oft than not, like ruffians and trollops."

The hideous man rested an arm on the counter and leaned forward—looking *more* hideous with each approaching inch. "So, how you make living, eh?"

Klaus' eyes met the man's; the stranger's stare was almost hypnotic. "In point of fact ... I don't." It was, Klaus knew, a stupid thing to say; he'd never get away with charging a steep

33

Paul McComas & Greg Starrett

rate now. But somehow, this wily-looking horror had a way of pulling the truth right out of him. "*Meine tochter* and I are recent arrivals here."

"Your daughter," said the other with a nod, "ye-e-e-esss. Ygor see her leave as he come in." His dark eyes sparkled. "Very ... lovely, eh?"

Klaus wasn't sure whether to thank the creature, or punch him—so he ignored the comment and continued: "When my wife passed away, we left Vasaria to—"

"Vasaria?" The weird man's eyes lit up. "You live zhere—tailor zhere?"

"We lived there, yes. But I worked at ... at the brewery. And I don't even drink beer! I'm an oenophile."

The man raised a bushy eyebrow. "It, eh, none of Ygor's business if tailor happen to like—"

"*Wine!*" Klaus cut in, deeply offended. "It means that I am an aficionado of wines, and of the finer spirits." His eyes narrowed. "Yet there I labored, day after endless day, in the village brewery, just as my father did, and his father before him." In his head, the speech continued: *And I came home each night smelling of yeast and hops—just as they did, in their day. And being called, by one and all, "Hops-schmidt"—just as...*

"So, you not *real* tailor?"

Klaus stepped toward him; the next words came shooting out in an ice-cold stream: "Let me make one thing clear. I am the most skilled tailor in the entire province—quite possibly in all of Europe. I threaded my first needle at nineteen months; I took my first measurement the very day that I learned to count. Over the years, I came to outfit many of this nation's most notable men; why, I've clothed the Kaiser himself! But all of this, I did *on the side*—a 'hobby,' as it were—until my wife's untimely demise, seven months ago. In

Fit for a Frankenstein

the wake of that tragedy, and in the spirit of 'Life is short, so *carpe diem,*' I handed in my brewing apron and sold our house, and my daughter and I moved here, to begin our lives anew. As it turned out, the only problem, the only fly in the ointment of this, my grand, life-affirming scheme, is that the good people of Kotstadt seem to believe that they would have more use for a … an igloo-builder, or perhaps a narwhal-hunter, than they do for a tailor." Klaus caught his breath, then placed his small, nimble hands on his slender hips. "Now. Sir. Any questions?"

"Just vun: Can you make size, ehhh…" He threw up his hands. "…size 66-Extra-Extra-Long suit?"

Klaus eyed him warily. The man before him was no larger than he—and stood shorter, thanks to a crooked neck and slightly hunched back. "I can, but frankly, you'd be swimming in it."

"Is not for me. Is for … friend."

"Well then, your 'friend' will have to come in for a fitting."

"No!"

Klaus shrugged. "I'm sorry; it's the only way we can ensure—"

"*NO!*" The counter shook under the loud *thud* of the would-be customer's fist. "He no can come; he, eh … busy."

"Listen," said Klaus, "if I'm to do a job, then I must do it right. That means an initial fitting before I can begin, then a second fitting once the suit is in process, for alterations. Two fittings, one suit; *no* fittings—*no* suit."

Klaus' "tough customer" gave this some thought, then smiled. It was a jagged-toothed, horrible smile. "Ygor make you deal: *vun* fitting." He pointed at Klaus. "You, tailor-man, make size 66-X-X-Long suit; zen, Ygor bring friend in for, eh … alterations."

35

Paul McComas & Greg Starrett

Klaus paused, considering, but then shook his head. "I'm sorry..."

"Tell me, *Herr* Hauptschmidt: You in any position to turn down paying customer?"

One side of Klaus' mouth turned up. "A valid point. But I've yet to see any 'pay.'"

"Ygor ... no have money vith him now..."

With a scowl, Klaus turned away. "Nor anything of value for collateral, I'm certain."

"Oh, ye-e-e-esss."

Klaus paused, his curiosity piqued. He turned back to see the old unsavory pulling from his deerskin pouch a shepherd's horn. It was, in shape and design, unusual—weird, even—but hardly a treasure. "*This*, Crooked-Neck? This crude *shofar*, you offer me as 'collateral'?"

"Is no *chauffeur*; horn no drive Ygor around town! Is instrument: has finger holes—see? Besides, is Ygor's prize possession!"

And from the look on the other's face, the tailor knew that he was telling the truth—in which case, he would indeed come back to claim and pay for his order. Klaus drummed his fingertips atop the counter.

"You vant I should play it, Herr Haupt—?"

"Don't; please." The tailor snapped up the horn, weighing it in his hands. "And when you return, you ... *will* have money?"

"Oh, ye-e-e-esss. Ygor know vhere to get—er, vhere to *earn* money, fast. Lots of money."

"Very well," Klaus muttered, tucking the horn on a shelf behind the counter. From the same shelf, he then pulled out a thick, leather-bound sample book and set it down heavily on the counter top. "You must choose a color..."

"Black."

36

Fit for a Frankenstein

Klaus flipped the book to the middle. "...and a fabric."

The customer again threw his hands into the air. "Ze *best!*"

Klaus peered at him, then flipped over to a new page. "This tight-woven blend offers durability and heft, yet also breathes exceedingly well."

Ygor's mouth dropped open: "Ze fabric *breathes?* It's *alive?*" He placed an ear to the sample, listening.

Klaus rolled his eyes. "That is an expression. It means that your, uh, 'friend' won't get too hot."

"Even vhen ze light-en-ing strike?"

"What?" Klaus shook his head. "*What?*"

"Never mind." The crooked man tapped a fingertip against the fabric. "Is ze best?"

"Yes. Several of our nation's leading lights have worn this very fabric: Dieter Schnebel, the composer and conductor; moving-pictures actor Conrad Veidt; Baron Wolf von Frankenstein; General Otto—"

"Vait—*vhat?* After 'Veidt'!"

The tailor scowled. "'Vait, vhat, Veidt'—*excuse* me?"

The shaggy man stepped forward. "Vhat you say *after* 'Veidt'?"

"Baron Frankenstein?"

The other nodded, chuckling softly to himself. His voice, when next he spoke, was likewise low: "Ye-e-e-es. Ve use *zis* cloth. Is good enough for a Frankenshtein, is good enough for ... my friend."

"Very well." Klaus picked up a small notepad and a pen. "And what is your name?"

"Name ... Ygor."

Klaus could have guessed, but with this strange creature, it was hard to be sure. Meticulously, the tailor began to print: capital *I*...

37

Paul McComas & Greg Starrett

"Not *I*..."

"Not you?" asked Klaus, looking up. "Then who?"

"No," said Ygor, "is 'Ygor,' with a *vhy*."

"*Y?*"

"Vhy? Ygor not know vhy! Because Ygor's mother spell it zat vay!"

Klaus blinked twice, then resumed printing: "Ygor: *Y*, *G*..."

"Ygor already *tell* you vhy—and vhat you say 'Gee!' for? You surprised?"

"... *O* ..."

"Ah, so *now* you understand, eh? You say, 'Oh.'"

"...*R*. You—"

"Is Ygor *vhat?* Losing patience? *Yes*, Ygor losing patience—and do *not* ask 'Vhy'!"

For some reason, Klaus found himself recalling an American comedy duo he'd seen in a film at *Der Munich Moviehaus*. He shook off the thought and made another notation on the form, then said, "Size 66 X-X-Long jacket. And the waist?"

"Forty-eight."

"Inseam?"

"Fifty."

Klaus let out a low whistle. "Lucky for you this fellow's your friend; one would hate to have him as an enemy."

Ygor nodded. "Ye-e-e-essss. Vun vould."

The tailor looked over the figures before him and shook his head—"This job's going to be a real monster"—then set down his pen and ripped the top two sheets off his pad, keeping the original and handing over the carbon copy.

Ygor stared down at the estimated price. "Is a lot of money, eh?"

Fit for a Frankenstein

Klaus mimicked his accent: "Is a lot of fabric, eh?" Then, in his own voice: "One week, 'Mr.' Ygor."

"Too slow! Ve need sooner. Very soon!"

"Well, you'll pay extra for it: double that price, and you can have it in, oh, three days."

"And if Ygor vere to, eh ... *triple* ze price?"

Klaus could barely contain his excitement. It would be a long night—but it would be worth it. "This time tomorrow."

Ygor nodded. "Is good."

"Triple," reiterated Klaus, three fingers raised. "And not *ein pfennig* less."

"Yes, yes. Ygor vill pay." Then the strange figure turned and left the shop, muttering something to himself as the door slammed behind him.

Something that, to Klaus' dismay, sounded very much like:

"And tailor-man—*he* vill pay, too."

SIX
AWAY IN A MANGER

Dusk. The outskirts of Kotstadt. A light snow fluttered down on an understaffed and, thus, conveniently inconspicuous family farm, cloaking it in white.

As Ygor made his way through a gap between two askew rear planks and into the ramshackle barn, the sight that awaited him seemed at once familiar—and very wrong:

Surrounded by an assortment of curious livestock—a placid, lowing cow; two fluffy, *baaa*-ing white lambs; a friendly-faced donkey—the Monster, now clad in a rough-hewn blanket (plus his boots), knelt in the hay, cradling in its great, gangly arms a smelly, cloth-wrapped bundle ... and gazing down at its pungent prize with a look of purest adoration.

"Vhat he *have* zhere?" Ygor croaked to himself, then sniffed the air. "Is ... shtinky infant?" Squinting, Ygor stepped closer.

Inside the cloth: a big, half-eaten block of Limburger.

It was, all told, a nativity scene from Hell ... by way of Wisconsin.

Ygor lurched forward—"Baby Cheesus! Vhat you doing?"—and reached out...

"*NGAAAAR!*" The snarling Monster bolted to its feet, pressing the half-block to its chest; its other arm shot forward, shoving Ygor aside.

Ygor fell with a *thud* to the damp manger floor; he scrambled to his feet, shook himself, and swept the hay off his coat. "Vhy you do zat, eh? Ygor no take it; just vant to *see!*"

40

Fit for a Frankenstein

The Monster slowly shook its head ... then, one-handed, hefted the cheese to its mouth and took a fist-sized bite.

Ygor eyed his companion suspiciously. "Is vhat you vanted back in ze voods, eh? Instead of geeses and trout-fish: ze smelly cheese."

The Monster chewed mutely.

"Is 'tender and mild' now, but..." Ygor dropped his gaze to the Monster's slight paunch, and shook his head. "Is inside ze shtomach, and heading south. Ygor know all too vell vhat zat mean: soon, no more Silent Night! Zen, barn vill be *double*-shmelly. And vunce *zat* start, vell"—he gestured toward the surrounding farm animals—"Ve all dead here!"

The Monster swallowed, then half-smiled.

"You think is funny, eh? How funny it going to be when ve found out by ze farmer and his pitchfork, all because you shoot out ze gas, gas of a hundred men?" He pointed at the half-block. "Vhere you *get* zat, anyway? You break into village cheese shoppe?"

The Monster nodded, then took another bite.

Ygor folded his arms. "Anyvun see you?"

The Monster shook its head.

"Zat ze first *good* news Ygor hear." He sighed. "*Zis* what you doing while Ygor dealing with ze fuss-budget tailor, eh? And ordering for you ze finest of suits. Fancy suit; Frankenshtein suit! Suit zat vill cost Ygor vun pretty *pfennig*—" A thought ... then, a step forward—and a change in tone: "Eh, cheese shoppe ... it have cash drawer?"

The Monster shrugged, then took another bite.

"Of course it have cash drawer, maybe even a safe, vith many *marks* inside, just ... vaiting."

The Monster belched.

"Plus, with break-in earlier today, zey vill never suspect second vun tonight, vill zey?" Ygor cackled softly. "Is

Paul McComas & Greg Starrett

goooood." Then, hands raised like a pair of white flags, he stepped forward.

The Monster, though wary, permitted his approach.

"You, eh, you vant *another* cheese block, my friend? Vhen zis vun all gone?"

The Monster nodded.

Slowly, Ygor reached up—"Ve go get ze cheese, and *more*, after store close tonight"—and patted his companion's arm ... in the process accidentally nudging the wrap off the creature's shoulders. The blanket fell to the manger floor—and Ygor gasped:

The last scraps of its old suit now gone, the Monster—all seven-feet-plus of him—now stood before Ygor wearing nothing but its boots.

The cow stopped lowing.

The lambs stopped *baaa*-ing.

The donkey's jaw dropped open.

"Agh!" Ygor slapped a palm to his forehead, then closed his eyes tightly and turned away. "Ygor reeeally not need to see *zat!*"

SEVEN
MEANWHILE, BACK AT HAUPTSCHMIDT TAILORS...

Early evening. Having completed a series of arithmetical calculations regarding the dimensions of the suit for his latest (and, at present, only) customer, Klaus Hauptschmidt now furiously gathered up the supplies he would need to make it. He scurried about like a worker bee, collecting not pollen but needles, thread, patterns, and pins, then dashed into his storeroom and stacked atop his outstretched arms several bolts of the fine-yet-durable black fabric that Ygor had chosen. Klaus hustled the bolts into the work area of his shop; he was just beginning to unroll one of them onto his work table when his teenage daughter ambled in, two small pieces of marzipan candy in hand. She offered one to her father, who declined. "I'm too busy for snacks, *Tochter*. Busy, busy, busy as a..." He drew a blank and looked up. "Some manner of industrious insect. An ant, perhaps?" Klaus shook it off and returned to his work.

Gretl popped both candies into her mouth and spoke while chewing: "You say, *Vater*, that this man will pay you triple if you can get his job done by tomorrow?"

He reached for his best fabric shears. "Yes, my dear: triple."

"How much did he put down as a deposit?"

Klaus thought for a moment. He had taken no down payment for this work, with the exception of Ygor's horn— yet he hated to admit this to his daughter. He was desperate for the money; besides, deep down, he *knew* he would see his shaggy customer again. "He paid me half up front, Gretl."

43

Paul McComas & Greg Starrett

Her brow furrowed. "But *Vater*, there is no money in the register."

Klaus was now becoming annoyed, for he had many hours of work ahead of him and wanted to get started. "I put it in a safe place, my dear." He waved the shears in her direction. "Please, stop asking silly questions and go put some coffee on; it's going to be a long night."

Appearing a bit startled by her father's tone, the girl turned away, blonde pigtails whirling—"Very well"—and stepped back into the small kitchen behind the shop. Then she added, just loudly enough for him to hear: "No need to get your neck out of joint about it!"

* * *

Klaus had just finished cutting all of the material for the trousers—more fabric, by far, than for any pair of pants he'd ever made—when he heard a pair of loud noises coming from outside the shop. He stood and peered out the window, but it was dark, and all he could see was a fringe of falling snow illumined by the full moon. He shook his head. *Hope they aren't having more trouble at Wolter Cheese Shoppe!*

Earlier in the day, Klaus had taken a stroll through the village and overheard two of the other merchants discussing a break-in at Wolter's, which was located just across the cobblestone street from Hauptschmidt's.

Trouble for the cheesemaker, Klaus had fretted then, *could mean trouble for the tailor.*

The same thought returned to him now. But after several seconds and no further noise, he sighed, then sat back down and returned to his work. His left foot expertly working the pedal of his trusty treadle machine, Klaus began sewing the seams—the incredibly *long* seams—of the right leg. He

44

Fit for a Frankenstein

allowed himself a half-smile as he murmured, "These seams *seem* to go on forever."

He had just about finished his initial work on the right leg when Gretl arrived at his side with a large beer stein, brimming with black coffee. "I figured that a cup probably wouldn't be enough."

"You figured right, *Liebchen*." Klaus grabbed the handle and raised the stein as if in a toast. "This is good, for starters—but I hope you made a full pot, my child!" He took a sip.

"I did, *Vater*. And I made it extra-extra-strong."

Klaus nodded his approval. "Let's hope it's enough to get me through this size 66 extra-extra-long!"

EIGHT
DAS HEIST

The ever-canny Ygor had it all figured out—had, in fact, just spent a goodly chunk of time figuring it out: a cunning, elaborate scheme by which he and the Monster (now clad in a jumbo-size burlap produce sack with improvised neck-hole) could jimmy the lock of the loading entrance to the warehouse next door and clandestinely make their way, via a shared second-floor balcony, into the heavily bolt-locked Wolter Cheese Shoppe ... all with nary a disturbance nor sound.

Ygor therefore erupted into a string of half-whispered epithets and curse words when the Monster strode right up to Wolter's front entrance door, broke it off its hinges, and hurled it with a mighty *CRASH* into the store.

As the Monster lumbered inside, Ygor turned his upper body to steal a worried glance behind them, then scurried in after, berating his friend in a stage whisper: "Volter may live right upstairs; you think he not hear zat and vake up? Now he come down, vith gun! Voltage may be good for you, but Volter no good for Ygor!"

The Monster, presently slamming a series of small cocktail-size wedges—Milbenkäse, Tilsit, Weisslacker—into its gaping maw, paid no heed to its companion, nor to anything else non-cheese-related.

Ygor scowled, then quickly cased the joint and located, behind the counter, the door to a small wall safe. "Here, my friend!" he half-shouted, pointing. "Here, zey keep ze *mutterlode*: ze richest, tastiest, shtinkiest cheese in ze vorld!"

Fit for a Frankenstein

The Monster paused, analyzing (to the extent that it could) its caretaker's words. Then it turned and began lurching over to Ygor's side...

With a cacophony of barks and snarls, a massive *Wolfshund* came tearing down the staircase at the rear of the Shoppe, heading straight for the two intruders.

Despite his age and disability, Ygor nearly leapt up onto the counter. "Vorse zan gun!" he bellowed, eyes wide, from his roost. "Ygor survive bullets of Volf-Doctor—barely; not vish to try bite of Volf-*hound!*"

The Monster spun around to confront the livid, nearly-lycanthrope-size watch dog, matching the beast's throaty growl with one of its own.

From a remove of several feet, the two regarded one another with narrowed eyes: shoulders tensed, hackles raised, teeth bared, both preparing—and daring each other—to strike.

Then the dog stopped snarling; it took one trembling step backward, then a second. Tail tucked between its legs, it began to whimper.

Ygor, mystified, shook his head ... but then *he* smelled it, too.

Palms out, The Monster half-shrugged.

With a baleful cry, the *Wolfshund* spun around and dashed out the front doorway.

"Of course!" Ygor cackled, waving a hand in front of his face. "If shtink zis bad for Ygor, must be *torture* for dog!" Then he clambered back down to the floor. "Come, my friend. Ve have no more time to vaste." He pointed down at the safe. "Break in here for *über*cheese, *now!*"

The Monster bent over, took hold of the handle, and tore the safe's metal door off its hinges.

Inside: two stacks of *marks.*

47

Paul McComas & Greg Starrett

Before the Monster could register its disappointment, Ygor's hands darted in, each one grabbing a stack, and—with a cry of "Yoink!"—just as swiftly withdrew.

"Now, ve get out of here before ze townspeople come vith zheir torches." As he stuffed the cash into his pouch, Ygor's voice darkened: "How I hate ze townspeople vith zheir torches. Come!" And he reached out to tug at the edge of his companion's burlap sack.

But the Monster, ensconced beside a great mass of soft, drippy cheese, would have none of it: boots planted, the creature tore at its buttery prey with both hands, gorging itself.

Ygor sighed, then reached for his horn—but it was *gone!* "Ach," he croaked, "of course: Ygor give horn to tailor-man! How Ygor call friend away from here now?"

The creature continued to feed.

"Ah—Ygor know how!" And, seizing the platter that held the drippy cheese, he backed quickly away.

"*NGAAAAR!*" Arms raised, the other followed.

"Ye-e-e-esss!" Ygor retreated toward the missing front door, his familiar matching him step for step. "Zat's good!"

They emerged back onto the snow-covered street, then vanished into the darkness.

"Zat's riiiight," Ygor cajoled, platter still upheld, heading for the farm. "Monster—follow Münster!"

NINE
ALL-NIGHTER

Seated at his machine, Klaus turned the hand wheel toward him, adjusting the needle height. He pressed the take-up lever, pulling the black thread off the spool and feeding it through his trusty apparatus.

Then he reached for his stein, yanked it to his lips, took a great gulp of coffee and set it back down.

He adjusted the tension regulator, getting the pinch pressure just right. He set the stitch selector to the finest, tightest stitch, and he rotated the stitch plate into place.

Then he grabbed the stein and took two more gulps.

He depressed the presser-foot, engaging the tension discs, and reached to flip open the bobbin cover.

Three gulps, in rapid succession. "Gretl!" Klaus hollered hoarsely, hefting the now-empty stein into the air. "More *kaffee.*"

"On the way," she called back from the kitchen.

Klaus set down his stein, his shoulders slumping. *An "all-nighter"—that's what the university students call it.* He stared at the black fabric before him ... his thoughts, now, turning equally dark. *He* had wanted to go to university, once. He'd been accepted, too, at Tübingen—and from there, he'd always imagined, it would have been off to Switzerland, to study with Dr. Carl Jung. He, Klaus Hauptschmidt, could have been a pioneering psychoanalyst, a practitioner of the bold new "talking cure." He could have healed broken spirits, sewn back together tattered minds.

But his parents had called it "hogwash."

So, instead: Vasaria Brewery—and "Hops-schmidt."

Paul McComas & Greg Starrett

Thanks a lot, Mom and Dad.

"May not be a doctor," he mumbled to himself, "but I can still be the best damned tailor in the Western Hemisphere!" And, straightening, he placed his foot back on the treadle.

His nightgown-clad daughter appeared at his side, steaming coffee-pot in hand. But Gretl hesitated to refill the stein; perhaps the sight of her father—bloodshot eyes, drooping lids, pasty complexion—gave her pause. "Papa, you are working yourself to a frazzle."

He picked up the stein and waved it back and forth in front of her, like a prisoner scraping his tin cup against jail-cell bars. "*Kaffee*," he croaked—his voice sounding, to Klaus' own horror, distinctly like that of his current crooked-necked customer! He cleared his throat. "Please."

Clucking her tongue, Gretl refilled the stein. "You should sleep."

"No, *Tochter*." Klaus took a long, slow slip, then set the stein down. "Not till it's done." Then he gave her a weak smile—"Done, sold ... and paid for."—and turned wearily back to his work.

Gretl shook her head, sighed, and turned away. "I swear, *Vater*," she said, heading off to bed, "this job will be the death of you."

50

TEN
VHAT DREAMS MAY COME

The Monster, still clad in his produce sack, sat on the barn floor, leaning back against a hay bale, cradling—and continuing to consume—what remained of the Münster.

Ygor lay a short distance away, one palm resting lightly on his cash-filled pouch. It had been a long and eventful day— and, especially, night!—and slumber was now tugging at him. Weary eyes on his companion, he groggily asked, "My friend ... don't you ever sleep?"

The Monster merely raised a hand to lick the cheese off its fingertips.

Ygor half-chuckled, half-yawned, then began to sing: "Avaaaay in a manger, no crib for a bed ... Ze Frankenshtein Monster eat cheese vithout bread..." His voice was growing fainter with each line: "Ze stars, zey look down on his flesh cold and grey ... Ze Frankenshtein Monster pass gas in ze hay..."

He didn't make it to the next verse. For by then, Ygor was somewhere else entirely...

* * *

His eyelids opened slowly, heavily, to reveal some kind of laboratory—an unfamiliar one, neither Wolf von Frankenstein's nor that of Wolf's father, Heinrich. It was newer than either, and tidier. Ygor also realized that he was viewing his surroundings from a different perspective: his neck was upright for the first time in years, and he seemed to be looking out from a higher vantage point than normal. As

Paul McComas & Greg Starrett

he turned to see more, his legs and feet felt heavy, sluggish. He raised his hand into his field of vision—and reeled back in amazement: the hand was enormous, the flesh was greenish-grey, and scars from old stitches encircled his wrist. *Zis not Ygor's hand; zis ... my friend's hand! But how?*

He swung back and spotted a large wall mirror in one corner of the room. He lumbered toward it and saw an image of the Monster where Ygor's own reflection should have been. Ygor raised his arm; the Monster raised *its* arm. Ygor raised one foot, and the Monster did the same. Then it dawned on him: *Somehow, Ygor's brain is inside body of his friend!* "Now," he rasped—the voice, at least, still his own— "I have ze strength of a hundred men! I cannot die; I cannot be destroyed. No vun can stop Ygor now!"

He began to hear many people in the distance, shouting. The sound was coming nearer, growing louder ... and now the room was going dark—*so* dark, in fact, that he couldn't see anything. Was he—blind? He heard the sound of a door being battered down, then more shouting, very close. He turned and knocked over a shelf, heard the glass breaking— and felt sudden, intense heat. He could hear the crackle and hiss of a blazing fire. *Ygor must get out of here—but even vith ze flames, Ygor still cannot see!*

He stumbled around the room but succeeded only in knocking more things over. All the while, the fire grew ever larger, ever hotter. Ygor felt his skin—his *friend's* skin?— begin to blister, then heard a loud cracking above; with a *CRASH* of wooden timbers he found himself thrown to the floor, pinned there by a great weight. Ygor opened his mouth to scream and—

His mouth froze. His *face* froze—then his head. Enveloped in a bone-piercing cold, his entire body went instantly numb. *How could zis be? I vas so hot, and now—!* He

Fit for a Frankenstein

tried to move but couldn't, his limbs, head, and torso all held fast. He heard muffled pounding, felt the vibration with each blow. *Vhat ze hell is going on?*

Suddenly he felt a rush of warmth on his face. Ygor drew in a deep breath. He slowly opened his eyes: He could see again!—but very little, just the vague silhouette of a tall man facing him, chipping away with a large rock at the force holding Ygor. The more the man pounded, the more Ygor was able to feel ... and begin, just barely, to move. He felt the man reach in—desperately, it seemed—and start to free Ygor's arms.

Ygor now realized his predicament: *Ygor is frozen in ice, like ze black valnut in ze ice cream!* But this clearly troubled man before him was now helping him *out* of his frosty tomb. *Vonder vhy he helping?* Ygor tried to ask, but no sound came from his throat.

"I'm Lawrence Talbot," his deliverer said in a rumbling baritone. "Can you help me find Dr. Frankenstein's records?"

Frankenshtein's records? Ygor thought. *Doctor not even own ze phonograph!*

Then he found himself somewhere else. He felt stronger than he had after leaving the ice, and his eyesight was continuing to improve: he could see that he was in yet another laboratory.

Seemingly out of nowhere, he heard snarling, loud and fierce, and was thrown to the ground by some kind of large animal! *Another* Volfshund? He struggled to his feet to see a growling two-legged beast lunging at him again. *Vorse zan* Volfshund: *Verevolf!*

As a boy, Ygor had heard stories of such creatures, but he'd never thought them true; now, he quickly became a believer. He raised his arms, grabbed the furry fiend by its

53

Paul McComas & Greg Starrett

scruff—*Heel, boy!*—and threw it back into a large table. *Ha!* *"Fido" no match for me!*

The lupine brute leapt atop a large piece of lab machinery; Ygor pushed equipment and animal alike out of his way—then heard the sound of a muffled explosion and rushing water. He tried to grab hold of something to steady himself, but a wet wall engulfed him, its mighty force sweeping him away into—

Blackness. And, again, numbing cold.

He opened his eyes to see light dancing off the ice that, once more, was encasing his body. *Ygor not live in Arctic Circle; vhy he keep vaking up "on ze rocks?"* Straining to see outside his frozen prison, he identified the source of the dancing light: Fire. *My friend think "Fire bad," but if Ygor vait, zis fire vill varm him ... and* free *him.*

Pushing against the chilly walls that encased him, he could hear cracks forming—but he quickly exhausted himself with the effort. And so, he waited, staring through the ice at the hopeful light of the distant fire...

...which became a blazing torch thrust up into his face! Ygor stumbled backward: *My friend right after all—fire very bad!*

He panicked, mind racing; his worst fear had returned to torment him, for there were angry, shouting men all around him, each one carrying a horrible ball of flame on a stick. Reeling back, Ygor saw that he was outside some kind of castle—and that he had the limp body of an old man tucked under his arm. *Who ze hell is zis?*

He thought of dropping the body, but something drove him to hang on. As the men with torches converged upon him, Ygor carried his feeble companion down a set of huge stone steps, away from the castle and into the night—the mob following close behind. He had to get away from those

Fit for a Frankenstein

torches; he *had* to keep moving. *Vhy I don't just let zis geezer go? I vould be able to move faster!* He looked down into the old, pained face, and he somehow knew that this man had once been kind to him.

Suddenly Ygor heard a crackling sound and found himself surrounded on three sides by a wall of fire. *Ze whole vorld is burning!* He moved in the only direction available to him as the flames licked at his heels. Finally, the old man tucked under his arm spoke: "Don't go this way: quicksand! Quicksand!"

But Ygor barely heard these words through his own desperation to escape the fire. Another step—and the ground gave away under his feet! It was as if the earth itself had grabbed his waist like a mighty fist and was now pulling him down. The more he struggled, the tighter its grasp—and the deeper into the mire he plunged. His eyes were about to get sucked under, yet for some reason he felt compelled to raise up his old friend's head, as high as he could. *Is "sink or svim!" Ygor sink, but maybe Gramps here can—*

A dark silence.

Then, the sound of trickling water.

Ygor sensed that he was lying on his back. He felt as if a heavy, wet blanket were covering him from head to toe. This new place—wherever it was—appeared to be pitch black, very musty, and fairly warm ... certainly not frozen. *At least Ygor not ice-cream bar again!*

He heard voices drawing near, and he thought that he recognized one of them. He tried to make out what was being said but only caught bits and pieces of the conversation. One of the men held a light to his face, and it was then that Ygor could see his own body—no, his *friend's* body, still—covered in mud, with a skeleton at its side. He

Paul McComas & Greg Starrett

thought back to his last misadventure and concluded: *Ze bones must be Gramps.*

A feeling of unexpected sadness swept over him; Ygor tried to shake it off. *Ve must have been in ze mud a long time. Vell, at least is supposed to be good for ze complexion.* Then he felt one of the men take his hand, opening it as if for inspection and then letting it go. With great effort—he was now very weak—Ygor slowly re-closed his fingers. The men started to walk away, and Ygor tried to cry out: "No, don't leave me here; *help* me!"—but the only voices audible were those of the two men, now trailing off into the darkness.

Then Ygor found himself standing in ... of course: yet *another* laboratory!

He sighed and rolled his eyes: *Vhy not I find myself ever in nice hotel, getting ze room service?*

But at least he felt strong again. Before him stood two men. The shorter one had his back to Ygor, but just from the sound of this man's voice, Ygor was overcome with the same strange bond of friendship he'd felt for the now-skeletal "Gramps." The other, taller man was dressed in a fancy suit and tie—and was pointing a handgun at Ygor's newest comrade.

Ygor peered closely at the taller man's face. *Zat is ze music buff, who broke ice vith ze rock—ze guy who vanted to play* Herr Doktor's *records! Name is, eh, Talbot. Vhy he vish to hurt Ygor's new friend ... and vhy he now have mustache?*

Talbot fired a shot into the shorter man, who took a few steps toward him; Talbot fired again. Ygor looked on in horror as the shorter man collapsed to the floor.

Filled with a sadness and rage he could not comprehend, Ygor started toward Talbot. *Ygor kill you! Ygor avenge Shorty!* But he bumped into a shelf; several bottles of fluid fell off, shattering on the floor and igniting a raging fire. *Vhy*

Fit for a Frankenstein

zese labs alvays full of flammable materials on high shelves in easy-breaking bottles?

Talbot pushed over a second shelf, containing many *more* such bottles, and sent it crashing right into Ygor. Then something exploded, and Ygor was surrounded by flames. Once again he felt his flesh blistering, and just as before, a large beam crashed down from above, pinning him to the floor of the lab as he writhed and bellowed in searing pain...

* * *

Ygor opened his eyes:

His rustic surroundings were illumined by moonlight streaming in through the barn window above.

A loud snoring sound came from nearby; he stood quickly to see the Monster sleeping peacefully in the hay. Ygor looked down at his own hand: a weathered, regular-sized, unstitched human hand. Double-checking, he brought that hand back toward himself and rapped his knuckles three times against the bony ridge of his broken neck:

Knock, knock, knock.

A great relief swept over him. "Vas only a dream," he mumbled. He laid himself back down on the barn floor. "And vhat a dream!" Ygor's brow furrowed as he pondered the ramifications. "Vun thing clear: if everything Ygor saw— Ygor *becoming* ze Monster, zen fire, and deep-freeze, and flood, and re-freeze, and thaw, and quicksand, and ze moldy cave, and zen fire *again*—if all of zat vill truly come to pass, vell..."

He shook his head, and his crooked vertebrae crackled.

"Zat vill need to be vun hell of a durable suit!"

ELEVEN
ASLEEP AT THE WHEEL

Gretl Hauptschmidt rolled onto her back, yawned, stretched, and opened her eyes to a new day. A *bright* new day: sunshine streamed through her bedroom window, bathing her young face in a warm glow. "Weather's turned again," she mumbled, then pushed aside her blanket and heavy quilt, rose to her feet, moved quickly to the glass, and looked out:

Yesterday's snow was mostly melted, and the sunny streets of Kotstadt were lined once again with frost-free maples, boxelders, and chestnut trees in full autumn glory—thick-trunked, two- and three-story-high bouquets of orange, crimson, and gold.

My favorite kind of autumn, Gretl thought: *a real "Gypsy summer."*

She said aloud, "It's going to be a *wunderbar* day!"

Into the *waschraum* for her morning toilet, out of her nightgown and into a clean dirndl dress—the lowest-cut dress she owned, for yes, later today she'd be seeing Franz!—then a brief stop at the mirror to check her braids before whirling out of her room and into the hallway. "*Guten morgen, Vater!*" she trilled to his half-open bedroom door.

No response from inside—nor from downstairs.

This was a first: Papa *always* rose before she did, cooking breakfast-for-two and readying a tailor's shop that typically greeted more disappointment than customers. Traditionally, she then rose, made his bed for him (Klaus liked the way she did corners), and joined him downstairs for pastries, poached eggs, and hot *kaffee*...

58

Fit for a Frankenstein

"Papa?" She opened his door the rest of the way and stepped inside:

His bed was still made—with *her* corners.

Gretl sighed. "*Vater, Vater...*"

She found him, of course, downstairs in the work area: seated at his machine, snoring lightly, legs askew, one palm resting on the hand wheel, his torso sprawled across the sewing table at what looked to be a most uncomfortable angle. He probably hadn't been dozing for long, because there beside him—seemingly complete, and suspended from high on the wall like some great, black tapestry—was the most gigantic suit Gretl had ever seen.

"He did it," she said under her breath. "He really, truly did it."

A chronically light sleeper, Klaus stirred at the words. "Mmm ... Seidel?"

"Gretl, Papa. It's Gretl." She reached to touch his arm.

Klaus started to straighten, then winced in pain and yanked a palm up to the back of his neck. "Ow!" Crookedly, he cast a sideways glance up at his daughter.

She pointed at him. "You look like that Yg—"

"Don't say it," he muttered. With some effort, Klaus stood. "I don't want to hear that name, ever again—especially not after last night."

"Yes, but *Vater*, look: you finished the suit!"

"That I did, Gretl; that I did." Her father placed a hand to his eyes, only then noticing the silver thimble still ensconced over his left forefinger. He yanked it off and set it down, then spoke again, his voice rising with each phrase:

"Yes, I finished it. Now, let the 'gentleman' who ordered it come back in here and claim it, and *pay* for it, in full, and *present* it to this much-ballyhooed 'friend' of his—along with a box of Belgian chocolates and a sprig of *Gott*-damned

Paul McComas & Greg Starrett

edelweiss, if he so pleases ... and then, let the likes of him never darken our doorstep again!"

TWELVE
MAJOR ALTER(C)ATIONS

The sun rose higher, the birds sang sweetly, and the villagers began their day's work ... but Klaus grew more concerned with each passing hour. By noon, he was drumming his fingers on the counter; by one o'clock, he was pacing the floor; by two, he was turning Ygor's worthless-looking horn over and over in his hands, uttering a low (and somewhat horn-like) groan. Just after three—the sun now having clouded over, with a storm bank moving in fast—Klaus looked over at his adjustable sewing mannequin and asked it, under his breath: "Did I just get *bambüzled*?"

Her chores done, Gretl skipped through the shop and straight to the front door.

As lovely as a woodland nymph, Klaus thought. *A regular Daphne.* He set down the horn. "One moment, *Liebchen*."

Hand on the knob, she turned back toward him. "Yes, *Vater*?"

He eyed her cleavage. "I see you have a date."

She folded her arms over her chest. "Very funny."

"That same boy?"

"He's a young man, Papa. You would *like* Franz if you just gave him a chance."

"Would I?"

"Yes. The two of you have so much in common."

He stepped toward her. "Such as?"

"You're both ridiculously protective."

Klaus raised an eyebrow. "The jealous type, is he?"

"As a matter of fact ... yes." Gretl sighed, shook her head. "Papa, I can't so much as smile at someone else without Franz

61

Paul McComas & Greg Starrett

assuming the absolute worst. It's all 'Why did you do that?' and 'Stop flirting.' Oh, and 'It'll be over between us the instant another man touches you!'"

Klaus extended his forefinger and placed its tip to her shoulder. "Done."

Which made the girl smile. "Oh, Papa!"

"You've been dating this boy ... *how* long now?"

"Since Oktoberfest." She flushed—

—*no doubt,* her father thought, *at the memory of some secret intimacy.* "Only a month," he mused aloud, "yet already he's acting possessive."

"Well ... He says it's a sign of his love."

"More a sign of insecurity, if you ask me," Klaus pronounced—his inner would-be-psychoanalyst coming to the fore. Then, to himself: "The lad probably possesses an inordinately small—"

The door swung open, into the room, nearly clipping Gretl even as she leapt back: "Oh!"

And there he was. Grinning that ghastly grin—as thunder sounded somewhere behind him.

"Mr. Ygor," Klaus intoned, "come in. My daughter was just leaving. Gretl, you've a date, don't you?"

She needed no further inducement.

Ygor stepped aside as the girl departed. Then, loitering in the doorway, he swiveled his crooked body around to watch her go.

Klaus noticed this ... and also noticed, with chagrin, the precise target of his unsavory customer's gaze: Gretl's pert buttocks, perfectly defined beneath the thin fabric of her dirndl dress—and, furthermore, quickly dampening in the nascent rain. "Come *in!*" the tailor harshly reiterated.

Still watching the girl, Ygor chuckled. "Is 'Gretl,' eh? Like in ze fairy story with Hansel. Ze forest-vitch vant to *cook*

62

Fit for a Frankenstein

Gretl, because..." At last, he turned to Klaus. "...she, eh, good enough to eat."

Ein, svei, drei ... Klaus took a deep breath. *Get the money and give him the goods;* then *throw him out on his ear.* "I have your suit—er, your friend's suit—right here." He gestured back to where the massive garment hung, nearly filling the wall behind the counter.

Ygor's eyes lit up. "Ye-e-e-es, looks goooood!" He stepped forward. "Let Ygor see. Up close," he wheedled. "Let Ygor ... hold."

"You hold the suit when I hold the money."

"Ze money! Of course." He drew from his pouch a thick roll of *marks* and handed it over—his hand grazing that of the tailor.

Klaus shivered—and not just from the touch: he had a fair idea of where this money had come from. *But,* he told himself while beginning to count, *I have obligations to my young one—hopefully for some time to come, this "Franz" character be damned.*

"Is all zhere." A raspy laugh. "Ygor cheat death, but he no cheat tailor-man!"

Klaus looked up questioningly, then self-instructed: *Let it go.* "Yes," he said, slipping the roll into his vest pocket as a clap of thunder reverberated outside. "It all seems to be here."

"My horn!" croaked the other.

"With pleasure." Klaus quickly handed it to him.

Ygor slung the horn's strap around his shoulder, tucking the instrument against his side.

"Which leaves only the matter of the final fitting. And a vital matter it is: for all we know, major alterations could be required." Klaus gestured toward the doorway. "Your, uh, friend will be joining us?"

"Oh, ye-e-e-es," the other grinned. "'Vill be.'"

Paul McComas & Greg Starrett

A crackle of lightning from beyond the window.

"But first…" Ygor gestured for Klaus to hand him the suit. The tailor complied.

Ygor laid the gigantic garment atop the counter and set about inspecting it at close range. "Goooood," he murmured, "very good, *Herr* Hauptschmidt. My friend, his size very big, but zis suit, it suit him. You sew ze pieces together vell—like a regular Frankenshtein." As more thunder sounded, Ygor held up one massive sleeve. "In fact, you better zan *Herr Doktor*: *your* stitches not even show!"

Klaus gave a curt bow. The man was hideous—but compliments, like customers, had been few and far between.

"I have question." Ygor turned toward him. "You see, my friend is, eh, outdoorsman. He real … rough-and-tumble kind of guy. Get into fights. Also into fires … floods … quicksand … he get frozen in blocks of ice. You know—ze usual."

Klaus, mystified, shook his head. "I…"

"But my friend, he … indestructible!" Cackling, Ygor lifted up a mammoth pants leg. "So, *suit* must be indestructible, too."

More lightning; more thunder.

The tailor nodded at his customer, then reached behind the counter. "For a modest fee, I can offer you *this*." He produced a small glass bottle equipped with a rubber squeeze-bulb—a free sample from those geniuses at the Black Forest Fabric Laboratory. "It's a highly protective synthetic coating. You simply spray it onto the garment's exterior, and—"

Ygor yanked the bottle away, sprayed it once into the air, and sniffed.

"It is virtually odor-free," Klaus informed him … but then caught wind of a most horrendous stench. "D-dear me!" the tailor stammered. "I, I assure you, it has never smelled like … like *that* before! A bad batch, no doubt." Klaus' eyes began to

Fit for a Frankenstein

water. "Oof—a batch from *Hölle* itself!" He shook his head sharply, yet the smell lingered. "I believe I have another bottle of it back here, so not to worry..."

"No," said his customer. "Ygor not vorried." Then he smiled. "But tailor should be. Shtink *not* from shpray-bottle; it from..."

The curtain separating Klaus' shop from his living quarters shot to the side.

"...*him*."

Klaus gasped. For there, stepping stiffly into *his own shop*, its flat-topped, ceiling-high head illuminated by a fresh crackle of lightning, was ... a nudemare.

"Agh!" Ygor slapped a palm to the side of his own face. "Vhat happen to your big potato sack?"

The Monster glanced down at its crotch.

"No, no—your, eh, burlap *covering!*"

The Monster shrugged.

Klaus had yet to speak; he tried, but seemed to have lost the capacity. Neck craned back, wide eyes locked with the Monster's heavily lidded ones, the tailor raised one trembling hand to point upward as his lips worked mutely away.

"Ye-e-e-e-es, *Herr* tailor," Ygor grinned, "*zis* my friend." And the twisted man slipped the bottle of protective coating into his pouch.

Needless to say, Klaus had more pressing concerns than this act of shoplifting.

"You probably vondering, 'Vhat should I call him?'"

Stepping back, Klaus stumbled, lost his balance; he dropped to one knee.

"Yes: *kneel* before him! For he have strength of a hundred men ... and yet, he have no name—zat is, until today. But now zat he get zis fine new suit, I *give* him name ... ze name he alvays deserve." Ygor turned, beaming, to gaze up at his

Paul McComas & Greg Starrett

friend. "You vere made by Dr. Heinrich Frankenshtein—no, not by vhat in Doctor's, eh, 'potato sack,' but by his hands, and by his *mind*. So zen, *you* Heinrich's son, just like Volf or Ludvig." His expression turned sour. "Remember zat annoying little curly-head Peter, vith his 'Vell, hel-*looooo*'? If *he* count as Doctor's kin, zen *you* do, too! So, even zhough you vere never born, my friend, you now must claim your birthright! And since you no can speak ... Ygor make claim *for* you."

The silent Monster blinked down at him, waiting.

Ygor cleared his throat, raised his arms, and boldly intoned:

"Now, you vill put on suit zat is fit for a Frankenshtein. And so: from zis day on, you vill be *known* as—"

The front door swung open; out of the storm and into the shop rushed Gretl, blonde braids awhirl. "Oopsy, forgot my umbrel—" Then she froze.

And all *Hölle* broke loose....

* * *

The eyes of men and Monster alike shot over to the buxom lass.

At last, Klaus' tongue came unglued—if clumsily: "Getl, gret *out!*"

But the girl, gaze locked on the looming Monster, rushed bravely forward, stopping where her father knelt. "Are—are you all right? Papa, what *is* that?" Hands on his shoulders, she leaned over him ... in the process providing for the gigantic figure before her a most impressive showcase.

The creature stared down. This girl was pretty; it had noticed that from the start. But now, given an eagle's-eye view of her cleavage, she quickly became the single most

66

Fit for a Frankenstein

glorious being it had ever seen. With growing excitement, the Monster began to sense or intuit or perhaps remember something important about women's breasts—something beyond their physical beauty:

Those—make—milk. And milk—make...

The Monster licked its lips.

Klaus gasped.

Gretl's jaw dropped open.

An oblong shadow *spanned* the Monster-adjacent wall.

And Ygor, shaking his head in grudging admiration, gestured up toward his friend. "Now ve see..."

Lightning. Thunder.

"...ze *true* size of Frankenshtein!"

Gretl rubbed her eyes, blinked twice—but the image remained, *filling* her field of vision. She thought, suddenly, of her young lover. To be sure, he was much more handsome than this stitched-up brute—but her father had called Franz a "boy," a "lad." Suddenly, Gretl found herself forced to agree.

For its part, the creature in front of her remained riveted on the prodigious jugs of its newfound Gazonga-Goddess. And the Monster, like her, now thought of someone else: that tall, stiff, high-haired, flinching woman the Doctor had constructed for it, so many years ago. The one called "Bride." She, the Monster remembered, had screamed at the mere sight of him ... but this girl wasn't screaming. And what's more:

Bride—not—look—like—these!

The Monster reached for the Dairy Section with both hands and grabbed on tight.

Now, Gretl *did* scream.

Klaus leapt to his feet and pulled his still-shrieking daughter out of the Monster's mitts.

67

Paul McComas & Greg Starrett

Ygor nabbed the suit from the counter and rushed toward his friend.

The Monster, fingers groping the air, advanced on Gretl.

Klaus pushed his daughter behind him. For lack of a weapon, he whisked his sewing mannequin off the counter, hoisting the wire torso like a bludgeon.

The Monster yanked the false figure away from the tailor—and tore it in two.

Klaus watched the dummy halves clatter to the floor.

"Ye-e-e-e-es!" Ygor hissed, his face lightning-lit. "See vhat my friend can do? Now, he do same to tailor-man!"

"No!" Gretl shrieked.

Ygor pointed at Klaus. "*You* no make 'major alterations' on suit, *Herr* Hauptschmidt; my friend here make zem—on *you!*"

A clap of thunder punctuated the threat.

Heart pounding, Klaus nudged Gretl toward the front doorway. "Go—get a constable!"

"But Papa—"

"Run! *Now!*"

The girl fled out into the storm.

The Monster strode forward, grabbed Klaus with one hand, and tossed him clear across the room, then lurched toward the front door.

Ygor caught his companion's arm: "No! You no can go out zhere into village ... not like *zat!* You lumber, not run; you too shlow for shtreaking." He began to help the Monster into its new suit. "Here ... ze pants, first." Getting them on proved challenging, given a certain stiff resistance. Ygor cursed, then complained: "You too much of good thing!"

Lying bruised on the floor, Klaus placed a hand to his forehead; he felt the warm ooze of blood.

"Zhere—finally! Now, ve *try* to zhip you up..."

Fit for a Frankenstein

Quietly, beneath a window streaked by the driving rain, Klaus got to his feet.

"...Good! Next, ze shirt..."

Klaus began edging toward the back exit.

"And, last: ze jacket. *Ach*—sleeves too short, again! But zat all right; make you look taller. Is very, eh, flattering; all ze chicks vill svoon at ze sight of you." Ygor caught a glimpse of Klaus; he whirled around, eyes afire. "You, tailor-man, no go anyvhere!" He thrust out his palm. "Give back ze money now, or I have my friend *take* it back!"

A *BOOOOM* of thunder.

Klaus hesitated. *Where the* hölle *is the* gottverdammt *constable?* He reached into his vest pocket, pulled out roughly half of the *marks*, hurled the bills at his customer, and dashed out the back door.

Outside, amidst the storm sounds: the shrill ring of a police whistle.

"Ze law!" Ygor lamented to the Monster. "Ve no vant to deal vith zem." He scooped a smattering of bills off the floor, then grabbed his friend's jacket sleeve. "Ve go out through back, like tailor-man. Come—"

But the Monster resisted.

"Vhat more you vant, eh? You just get to second base! Come, my friend—*come!*"

Its palms upraised in supplication, the Monster gazed forlornly out the still-open front door—the one through which *she* had run. Grunting plaintively, its blunt features now morose, the creature reluctantly allowed itself to be guided away by its ever-loyal familiar ... but its thoughts lingered on someone else. A single tear worked its way down the Monster's cold, grey cheek, for somehow, it knew:

I—never—meet—girl—like—those—again.

THIRTEEN
ON ZE ROAD AGAIN

It was the fastest pack-up-and-move-out in Kotstadt history.

A light rain fell as Klaus—bandage-browed and a bit woozy from his injury of a few hours earlier—fitted a final box and then his valise into the side compartment of the two-horse carriage. He pulled the broad canvas tarp over the luggage, cupped a hand to his mouth, and called out toward his soon-to-be-former home: "Gretl!"

The girl emerged: no longer skipping, but stepping warily out the back door. Upon reaching her father, she handed him her duffel bag.

He tucked it safely away. "Any word from the Inspector while I was packing?"

"He says his men are still looking. But honestly, I'm not even sure he believes us."

"*What?*"

She reached to adjust her woolen scarf. "Neither of the constables actually saw your friend Ygor, *or* that ... thing. I'm pretty sure they all think we're both batty."

Klaus scowled. "Good riddance, Kotstadt," he muttered, then clambered aboard and offered the girl his hand.

Gretl took it, climbed up, and sat beside him.

Klaus grabbed the reins—but hesitated. "I know this must be hard for you, *Liebchen*. Leaving your boyfriend and all..."

Gretl waved his words away. "It would all be over with Franz anyway," she sighed, "as soon as he saw *these*." She shifted her scarf aside to reveal her cleavage.

70

Fit for a Frankenstein

Upon each of her *fräuleins*: five large purple grope-marks. Klaus shook his head. "We Hauptschmidts bruise *so* easily! Rest assured, Gretl: those will fade."

"I know." She tucked the scarf back in place. "Truth be told ... somehow, after all that happened today, I think of Franz, and I think I can do big ... er, better."

Though troubled by his daughter's pronouncement, her father smiled at the apparent reprieve: his beloved only child, it now seemed, would still be sharing his home for some time to come. The realization buoyed his spirits. "At least we have friends in Vasaria, eh? And family. It will be good to see your cousin Ilka again, won't it? And help her tend her goose flock?"

"I suppose. But Papa, what will *you* do there? Go back to the brewery?"

Klaus shrugged. "I'll try tailoring first, see if I can make a go of it back home." He patted his vest pocket, bulging with the *marks* he hadn't returned to Ygor. "I've a bit of a windfall to work with; that should buy us some time. But if those plans fall through and I find it necessary to become '*Herr* Hops-schmidt' once again, well then..."

"Papa." Gretl placed a hand on his knee.

He patted her hand with his own. "It's all right, dear one. There are worse circumstances that can befall a man than being compelled to brew ... and there are *far* worse smells than yeast. I know that, now." He straightened up in his seat and gazed determinedly forward. "And, so..."

His daughter, too, sat erect; she gave her father a brave smile. "And so."

Klaus flicked the reins: the horses' hooves clattered into motion, and the carriage began trundling forward.

Moments later, as they passed the "Now Leaving Kotstadt" placard and veered left toward a sign reading

Paul McComas & Greg Starrett

"Vasaria, 37 Km," Klaus took heart in a welcome sight: the late-afternoon sun forcing its way through the dispersing rain clouds.

What he *didn't* see, however, were the two stowaways—one of them hunched and shaggy; the other huge, hulking, and nattily dressed—now silently ensconced amidst the luggage in the cart just behind him.

"Back to Vasaria," Klaus Hauptschimdt called out merrily. "Where at least there are no monsters!"

AUTHORS' NOTE

Thank you for reading our novella!

After all, without readers, a story—even one that's been published—goes untold. ("If a tree falls in the woods, and no one is there...") Readers are the electrical current that, when applied to a diverse assemblage of stitched-together body parts, animates and vitalizes said form; because you have read, visualized, and so experienced what the two of us have written, we can justifiably point to our modest tale and say:

"It's alive ... It's *aliiiive!*"

We certainly hope you've enjoyed our singular pastiche of humor, gothic horror, homage, parody, and quasi-historical fiction. (See, we *told* you it was made from diverse parts!) Perhaps you're wondering where in *Gott's* name such a bizarre story came from. There are two answers—one short, the other long.

The short answer is "From Leonard J. Kohl." See the excerpt of his essay on the 1942 film *The Ghost of Frankenstein* that serves as this book's epigraph (p. 11) and ends thusly: "Ygor, however, has managed to get the Monster cleaned up and gotten him a new suit by the time the weird-looking pair enters Vasaria."

Upon reading these words, Paul decided to fill in the gap by writing the story of how and where the Monster obtains his new garb—"the gap" being located within the fade-in/fade-out at the film's 0:08:42 mark. Paul also decided that this ne'er-before-told tale would be best told not by him solo, but in tandem with his friend of nearly 39 years and fellow now-grown-up "monster kid," Greg—who, to Paul's delight, quickly accepted the invitation to collaborate.

Paul McComas & Greg Starrett

Which leads us to the long answer: This story came from our shared, nearly lifelong love of the hauntingly atmospheric and monstrously fun Universal Pictures *Frankenstein* movies of the 1930s and '40s ... and from a friendship, soon to enter its (gulp!) fifth decade, whose history merits a semi-brief recounting here.

Take it, Greg:

"In the January 1974 issue (#104) of *Famous Monsters of Filmland* magazine, there was a small paragraph in the 'Classif-Hyde' ads which read as follows: 'CLUB: For LON CHANEY JR. For fans 12 & under. Many benefits. For info write President P.C. McComas.' Little did either of us know that this would lead to a long-term friendship that would produce a number of great projects, including this book.

"After writing to 'The President', I soon became a subscriber to his *Lonny Jr.* fanzine, the first of five eventual Macabre Publications (one of which, *Conrad*—devoted to actor Conrad Veidt—my friend Scott Merkel and I would put out on a semi-monthly basis). In December of that same year, my pen pal from distant Milwaukee came to stay at my house in Munster, Indiana, for several days, during which we made a short film together (as we were both budding filmmakers) called *The Invisible Man Meets the Wolf Man.* This really cemented our relationship, which continues to this day. There were indeed 'many benefits', as the ad stated, the best of which was getting to know someone who is now an old friend."

Take it, Paul:

"I paid tribute to my early friendship with Greg via the 'Craig Starling' character in my 2008 coming-of-age novel *Planet of the Dates*—but, as Greg says, our bond was not restricted to childhood; it's still going strong."

Fit for a Frankenstein

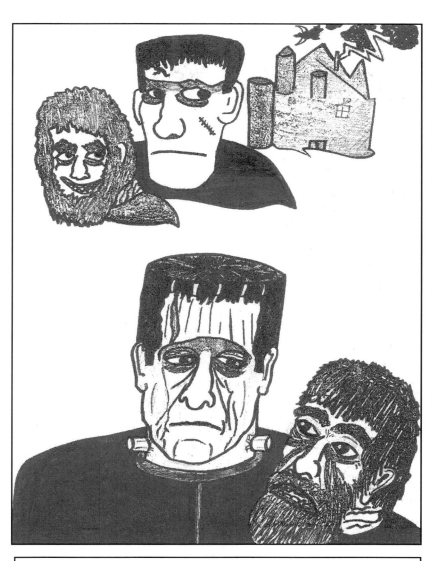

Paul's boyhood renderings of the disturbing duo; drawn at ages 11 (top) and 12, they ran in issues #3 (1973) and #12 (1974) of his 24-issue Lonny Jr. *fanzine.*

"What's more, with the addition of his wife, Laurie, and my wife, Heather, the duo evolved into a foursome. Greg and Laurie have been key members of my *No-Budget Theatre* (*NBT*) indie-film ensemble, lending their talents to seven installments (and counting)—on *both* sides of the camera. Most recently, the couple provided the premise, location, and makeup for—and also acted in—the 'In Search of ... Worm-Man' segment of *NBT #7: Gorzak's Grab Bag* (the script for which appears in my prize-winning 2011 Walkabout collection, *Unforgettable*). Greg and Laurie then proceeded to 'knock it outta the park' as Romulan Emperor and Empress Blagos in *NBT #8: Time Trek*.

"I've been able to repay the favor by serving as a voice actor in the Starretts' own Veidt Radio Theatre ensemble; among other parts, they gave me the plum role of a still-alive-at-age-1,800-plus Marcus Aurelius! So, let's see: Greg and I met through monster movies, then went on to make magazines, films, and radio plays together—but never a book. If only there were some way to address that omission..."

As you can see, it was all but inevitable that we join forces, ultimately, on *Fit for a Frankenstein*.

Once we did so, things went swiftly and smoothly. Paul began writing in mid-July 2012, just before midnight on—honest to God—a thunder-and-lightning-filled night. Numerous ping-pong-style volleys with Greg later (during which each of us provided valuable feedback on one another's sections), we put the finishing touches on Draft 1 in mid-October—a mere three months after we'd started. Revision occurred throughout the process, with a bit more in November, and *Voila! Fit* was finished.

But it wasn't always *Fit*. Initially, we "tried on" *The Suit of Frankenstein*, then the double-entendre-ready *The Size of Frankenstein*, but Greg—ever the stickler on this point—was

Fit for a Frankenstein

concerned that both titles reinforced the widespread public misidentification of the good Doctor's creation as "Frankenstein." (The name, used properly, refers only to the scientist and his kin.) It was Greg who finally suggested *Fit*, which Paul embraced—and we never looked back. (Ironically, while our story depicts a good deal of tailoring, at no point does either the Monster or anyone else actually obtain a fitting.)

Given the relatively modest scope of a novella, it's, uh, fitting (sorry!) that—aside from a guard dog, some forest fauna, and a few barnyard animals—only four actual characters appear in the book (not counting people about whom Ygor dreams): the Monster; his friend, Ygor, who is the star of our show; the tailor, Klaus Hauptschmidt; and Klaus' young daughter, Gretl.

In the case of the first two, we were "channeling" existing film characters whom we both have known and loved for years—and were picturing, in the process, two specific actors. It's hard to imagine anyone other than Bela Lugosi—who portrayed Ygor brilliantly in 1939's *Son of Frankenstein* and again in *The Ghost of Frankenstein* three years later—playing that part; thus, as we put Ygor through his paces, writing new scenes and lines for him, we both very much had "Bela on the brain."

Though Boris Karloff created (so to speak) the Monster by playing him/it to perfection in the first three films of the series, it was the bigger, bulkier Lon Chaney, Jr. whom we pictured in the role, since it was Lon who (rather stoically) played the part in *The Ghost of Frankenstein*—and the entirety of our narrative takes place within the timeline of *Ghost*.

As for Gretl Hauptschmidt, we weren't envisioning any particular actress but were aided by a mutual appreciation for

Paul McComas & Greg Starrett

buxom, braided young alpine blondes in frilly, low-cut dirndl dresses. (Gretl's goose-tending cousin Ilka, by the way, appears briefly in *The Ghost of Frankenstein*, played by Hollywood ingénue [and sometime Abbott & Costello co-star] Janet Warren.)

And then there's Klaus. We considered modeling the uptight yet lovable tailor on some noted character actor of the Lugosi/Chaney, Jr. era (Peter Lorre, Akim Tamiroff, George Zucco, etc.), but then went in the opposite direction and took our inspiration from the equally talented but *contemporary* actor David Hyde Pierce—specifically, from his four-time Emmy-winning work on the long-running TV show *Frasier*. This, as it turned out, worked like a charm; after all, who could possibly be more different from Ygor, or prove to be more flummoxed by him, than one Dr. Niles Crane?

Often, authors are asked, "What other books out there are like yours?" We're proud to report that, to the best of our knowledge, there is *nothing* out there quite like *Fit for a Frankenstein*; indeed, that's part of the reason why we wrote it! The novella is probably closest not to any other book, but to a movie: Mel Brooks' hilarious 1974 parody/homage *Young Frankenstein*—though our *Fit* is (for the most part) less over-the-top, and it sticks a bit closer to the source material that Brooks and we shared.

Speaking of that source material, one of the bonuses of writing this novella was that it required us both to revisit, yet again, most of the classic Universal Pictures *Frankenstein* movies we'd first watched on TV in our youth: the "Ygor double feature" of *Son* and *Ghost* in particular, but also (for the sake of Ygor's prescient dream in Chapter 10) the three films that *follow* that duo: *Frankenstein Meets the Wolf Man* (1943), *House of Frankenstein* (1944), and *House of Dracula*

Fit for a Frankenstein

(1945). Doing so was like reconnecting with a bunch of beloved childhood friends. (The gorgeous musical scores alone—by the likes of Franz Waxman, Frank Skinner, and Hans J. Salter—made the "reunion" worthwhile.)

What's more, in weaving our yarn—or, should we say, sewing our suit?—we managed not only to pay tribute to the Universal *Frankenstein* series, but to sneak in a few "lesser homages" as well. Surely, you caught the modified Abbott & Costello routine in Chapter 5 ... but how about the Chaney Jr.-inspired *Of Mice and Men* reference in Chapter 2? Or the there-for-no-particular-reason snippet of tailor-/"Taylor"-related dialogue from *Planet of the Apes* that immediately precedes the first meeting between Ygor and Klaus? *Frasier* fans likewise will find a nod or three to their beloved sit-com. "Easter eggs," the kids call 'em; happy hunting!

In addition, we'd venture that you just may have learned a word or *svei* of *Deutsch* along the way. (*We* did, anyway.)

And for all the numerologists (and superstitious folk) out there, consider: 13 chapters ... 13-point type ... 2013 publication. Beware of paper cuts—or, for you e-book readers, electric shocks—while turning these pages.

"But, wait; there's more!" While collaborating on *Fit*, inspired by "old Ygor" and with Halloween fast approaching, we wound up reworking a portion of Chapter 3 into a stand-alone, *non*-Frankensteinian flash-fiction horror piece, "After the Fall" (a.k.a. "Living Ghost"), that immediately follows this Authors' Note and closes out our slim volume with, we hope, a discomfiting shudder. Be forewarned: the tone here is darker than in *Fit*. "After the Fall" is best read alone, at night, by torchlight ... at the base of a gallows.

In closing, we both hope you've enjoyed *Fit for a Frankenstein*, our tale of a great friendship between Ygor and the Monster. It was all made possible only through a unique

Paul McComas & Greg Starrett

series of events which began with a long-ago ad, placed in a long-ago magazine, resulting in *another* great friendship— and, ultimately, in this book.

Paul McComas & Greg Starrett
December 2012

BONUS STORY: "AFTER THE FALL"
A.K.A. "LIVING GHOST"

He awakens to the odor of fetid water and human waste. Above him: an iron-barred window—and, streaming through it, the light of a new day.

His last day.

Bang ... bang ... bang...

He leaps up and, on tiptoes, peers out:

In the adjacent village square, three workmen put the finishing touches on a gallows.

The prisoner mutters a quick prayer.

Heavy footsteps echo in the corridor, then the door creaks open and two guards burst in. The taller one winks. "Here's where the fun begins."

They haul the condemned from his cell, then drag him—under the mockery of a blue sky—through the prison yard and into the square. He looks up:

High atop the platform, a black-hooded hangman reaches to adjust the noose.

Hustled through the crowd, the prisoner looks around in desperation at the familiar faces, hears the hateful cries:

"Fiend!"

"Villain!"

"Monster!"

"*Devil!*"

Another mumbled prayer—interrupted by the tall guard: "Our Lord don't hear the likes of you."

Paul McComas & Greg Starrett

Peering down, the condemned watches his own feet ascend the rickety steps: right, left, right, left. At the top, the noose is slipped over his head, followed by a black cloth sack that plunges him into darkness. "A miracle ..." he begs under his breath as someone recites the death sentence. A second voice: "Any last words?"—then a sudden *WHAM* as the trapdoor swings open and he plunges down and a jolt *rips* through his neck and then—

Nothing.

Clouds gather above, blotting out the blue. A light rain begins to fall.

"Cut 'im down."

The hangman draws his knife and, with three deft strokes, severs the rope:

The corpse hits ground with a *thud*.

A doctor approaches, kneels, and removes the sack, revealing the grisly evidence. He checks briefly for a pulse, looks up—"I pronounce this man dead"—then steps away.

The crowd draws near, hungry for a closer look.

Two men pull a small wagon up to the crumpled figure. Taking hold of wrists and ankles, they hoist it off the ground.

From the half-open mouth: a low gurgling sound.

They drop the body.

The deceased begins to cough. Moves one hand, then the opposite leg.

The villagers shriek, gasp—and draw near no more.

"He's alive!" cries one of the wagonmen.

The other crosses himself. "'Tis the work of the Fallen Angel!"

Slowly, painfully, the still-noosed figure before them gathers itself together. Bent-necked, misshapen and trembling spasmodically, it staggers to its feet. "Fallen?" it croaks, looking from one man to the other. "Yes." The ex-

Fit for a Frankenstein

prisoner jerks a thumb back toward the gallows. "But then, like Lucifer, I got ... back ... *up!*"

His raspy cackle ringing in their ears, the panic-stricken workers look helplessly at one another.

"Why, you're white as ghosts—but *I'm* the 'ghost' here, aren't I? Hanged"—he grips the noose—"yet, somehow, walking ..." He lurches toward the duo, who stumble backward. "And talking! You didn't *let* me speak before; hear me now."

Holding his broken neck as straight as he can, he turns to address the now-hushed townspeople:

"My sentence has been carried out, and the doctor's rather hasty pronouncement made: I'm 'dead.' You, however, *live* ... with a specter now in your midst. One that, being flesh and blood, cannot be exorcised or dispelled." He laughs. "Nor killed, it seems! A wraith that will haunt, bedevil, and torment you for the rest of your natural lives. Don't worry, though..."

He catches the eye of the tall guard who taunted him mere minutes ago, and gives the now-trembling man a wink.

"Here's where the fun begins."

ABOUT THE AUTHORS

Paul McComas (left) is the author of two novels and two short-story collections. His most recent book, *Unforgettable: Harrowing Futures, Horrors, & (Dark) Humor* (2011, Walkabout Publishing), won a Silver Prize at the 2012 Midwest Book Awards. His next novel, *Logan's Journey*, co-authored with *Logan's Run* author William F. Nolan, is slated for 2014 publication. Paul has edited two short-fiction anthologies, and his short indie movies have been screened at festivals worldwide, garnering international and national prizes. He teaches writing, literature, and film at various sites. A Milwaukee native, Paul lives in Evanston, IL, with his wife and fellow fiction writer, Heather, and their rescue greyhound, Sam. Info: **www. paulmccomas.com**

Greg Starrett (right) is a first-time author. He is a founder of Veidt Radio Theatre, which produces original Old Time Radio shows. Greg is also an occasional guest host and voice-over man for WJOB-AM 1230 in Hammond, IN. He is employed as a telecommunications technician and enjoys foraging for wild foods, making jellies, mustards, and pickles, and beekeeping. A native of "Da Region," he lives in Munster, IN, with his wife and best friend Laurie, their cat Tippecanoe, and dog Tyler too.

WALKABOUT PUBLISHING
Great stories by great authors.

Robert E. Vardeman—Michael A. Stackpole—Marc Tassin—James M. Ward
Lorelei Shannon—Dean Leggett—Kathleen Watness—Paul Genesse
Jason Mical—Kelly Swails—Sabrina Klein—Kerrie Hughes—John Helfers
Brandie Tarvin—Donald J. Bingle—Tim Wagonner—Anton Strout
E. Readicker-Henderson—Wes Nicholson—Linda P. Baker—Steven Saus
J. Robert King—Chris Pierson—Daniel Meyers—Elizabeth A. Vaughan
Richard Lee Byers—Jennifer Brozek—Brad Beaulieu—Dylan Birtolo
Paul McComas—William F. Nolan—Annette Leggett—Eric Greene
Stephen D. Sullivan—Jean Rabe—*And More!*

Pirates of the Blue Kingdoms • Blue Kingdoms: Buxom Buccaneers
Blue Kingdoms: Shades & Specters • Blue Kingdoms: Mages & Magic
Stories from Desert Bob's Reptile Ranch • Stalking the Wild Hare
Martian Knights & Other Tales • Luck o' the Irish • Carnage & Consequences
Zombies, Werewolves, & Unicorns • The Twilight Empire • Unforgettable
This and That and Tales About Cats • Uncanny Encounters: Roswell
Tournament of Death 1 & 2 • The Crimson Collection • *And More!*

Walkabout Publishing
P.O. Box 151 • Kansasville, WI 53139
www.walkaboutpublishing.com
Official Home of the Blue Kingdoms

Made in the USA
Middletown, DE
30 September 2015